THIS BOOK BELONGS TO

. . . .

. . . .

For my mother, Margaret ❧

First published 2008
by Walker Books Ltd
87 Vauxhall Walk,
London SE11 5HJ

10 9 8 7 6 5 4 3 2 1

© 2008 Charlotte Voake

Tweedle Dee Dee is the author's version of the
traditional folk song "The Green Leaves Grew Around",
which has no known writer or copyright holder.

The right of Charlotte Voake to be identified as the
author/illustrator of this work has been asserted by her
in accordance with the Copyright, Designs
and Patents Act 1988

This book has been typeset
in Charlotte.

Printed in China

All rights reserved

British Library Cataloguing
in Publication Data: a catalogue record
for this book is available from
the British Library

978-1-4063-0714-6

www.walkerbooks.co.uk

Tweedle Dee Dee

CHARLOTTE VOAKE

WALKER BOOKS
AND SUBSIDIARIES
LONDON · BOSTON · SYDNEY · AUCKLAND

ONCE in a wood
there was
a tree,

the finest tree
you ever did
see.

And the green leaves grew around around around,

the green leaves grew around.

AND
on that tree
there was
a branch,
the finest branch
you ever
did see.

The branch was
on the tree,
the tree was in
the wood,
and the green
leaves grew
around
around around,
the green leaves
grew around.

AND on that branch there was a nest, the finest nest you ever did see.

The nest was on
the branch,
the branch was on
the tree,
the tree was in
the wood,
and the green
leaves grew around
around around,
the green leaves
grew around.

AND in
that nest there
were some eggs,
the finest little
eggs you ever
did see.

The eggs were in the nest, the nest was on the branch, the branch was on the tree, the tree was in the wood, and the green leaves grew around around around, the green leaves grew around.

AND in those
eggs
there were some
birds,
ONE and TWO
and THREE!

"CHEEP!" went one.
"CHEEP!" went another,
and the third went,

"TWEEDLE
DEE DEE!"

The birds were in
the eggs,

the eggs were in
the nest,

the nest was on
the branch,

the branch was
on the tree,

the tree was
in the wood ...

and the green leaves grew
around around around.
And the birds went

"TWEEDLE
DEE DEE!"

THE TREE SONG